Columbus Park
A Brand New Start

— N E EVANS —

Chronicles of Nutwood Grove Series

Published by Valeant Press

Copyright 2018 N Evans

First published in 2018
Front cover by Shutterstock

ISBN:
Print: 978-0-9571009-6-1
iPub: 978-0-9571009-7-8
Kindle: 978-1-911412-82-3

Printed by Valeant Press Kimberley
Loughborough LE11 3AP

Valeant Press is an imprint of Dolman Scott Ltd
www.dolmanscott.co.uk

Contents

Foreword iv

Chapter 1
A Brand New Start 1

Chapter 2
A Worrying Encounter 5

Chapter 3
Familiar Friends 11

Chapter 4
Swamped 17

Chapter 5
Recollection 'A Nightmare' 21

Chapter 6
The Storm 25

Chapter 7
The Wolf of Liberty 29

Chapter 8
Larette 35

Chapter 9
Getting Settled 41

Chapter 10
The Snows of Winter 47

Foreword

The memories of the past few weeks still haunted Jobe, the reality was, that he was now alone. Scar had returned to the Mountains following the death of his dear partner Heti, who was laid to rest on an island surrounded by the ever flowing waters of the river. The red Mist had taken all that was dear to him; Jobe, who now has a new colony to mould and protect. Many friends had been lost and the whole eastern side of the forest was left burnt and blackened. Soon the humans will move closer as the need for housing grows, the pollution of the natural forest has already begun and life would never be the same.

Jobe had lost some fight since the passing of his dear mother, he was to be challenged over the coming winter, as food was sparse and humans move ever closer. Deacon had already fought his guilt with Jobe and he was tentative to say the least of his future. Soon the whole colony will need to stick together, new characters emerge, new challenges and tough decisions will test his resolve as we follow the continuing saga of Columbus Park.

In the mountains Scar was deeply saddened by the events of the last few days, he was worried that following the death of Heti. His son, so very young would not cope with the upcoming challenges. His life was here as the humans continue their quest for his head but he could not endanger the new colony but must be prepared to assist if needed.

Only time will really tell of how his son will cope but his own life is a challenge every year the annual hunt for him continues and as the humans obtain better weapons his demise grows ever closer.

Columbus Park
A Brand New Start

Chapter 1

A Brand New Start

As the rain eased Jobe took himself away from the colony to visit the last resting place of Heti, his beloved mum. It was quite a walk as they had moved on from where the red mist turned.

He sat contemplating across the water which surrounded Heti's grave. The clouds parted and the sun, so long, invisible, sat in the sky, but it was so very strange.

Never had the sun been such a colour, the sky had an eerie aura, sand whipped up by fierce winds in the south, drifted up and mixed with the remnants of the red mist still burning in the far east of the forest, though slowly dying out.

Jobe's mind drifted to past events, recalling all that was hurtful to him over such a short time. Many friends had been lost and sadness grew, their lives lost to the red mist, as yet, unable to confirm their demise or otherwise. Those who suffered such an agonising death would be remembered, those who survived will be thankful but haunted by the memories of the past.

Secrets were kept, but for the right reasons, though sadness cascaded in the heart of Jobe he was unsure if he would ever be fine. Being so young and following the trials of the past, he had an uncomfortable feeling of anxiety, all the expectations of the colony rested on the shoulders of a young inexperienced bear, who faced an uncertain future once they reach the new home.

"Gather round" Jobe said. " It is time to move on to a safer place. Most of the fires are out, but this will bring humans closer, so it is no longer safe here. In this part of the forest we are aliens at the moment, but if we stay together we will be fine. Deacon, you will be upfront with me, I can trust your sense of direction, as I am unfamiliar with the area. Limpy try and behave a bit, we will no doubt meet others along the way, since the fire I feel you have changed. Sadly Bonso got separated from us but we are unable to go and look for him. Let us hope he is fine and has found another stream. Arco and Jude can you bring up the rear, one of you mark each turn we make just in case we have to retreat at any time."

"Where are we going Jobe?" Jude asked. " Where has Scar gone? I thought he was back to look after us!"

"Jude, my father came to help with mum, he cannot remain here as the humans would still chase him, this would put us in danger. We are moving further into the forest, not as far as in the mountains where scar is. We need to be deeper in the forest to be safer, he will keep a distant eye on us and if needed he will come.”

“We are so far away from the places we all know, will the map help us any? but not sure it covers the whole area.”

“The Map yes of course.”

Jobe fumbled for the map, retrieving it from his pocket.

They all found shelter beneath the canopy and spread the map out. Jobe located North as they all studied the map, at times Jobe rubbed his chin as he deliberated where they were. Deacon pointed out the river Testament and where they lay Heti, they then traced the trail to where they were at that moment. Once this was established together Jobe and Deacon discussed the best and safest direction to travel.

Jobe noticed a small village not that far away from where they were, which worried him a little as his mum and dad told him to avoid humans, who would chase them away.

“We need to avoid this area, as much as we can, a human village is a dangerous place. If we go close to the village and divert this way, we should be ok.”

Deacon interrupted,

“We may have a problem here, look, I can remember this as being a swamp, which is an issue.”

“Mmm, yes, I see. We could go round the edge and just keep out of the main swamp, it would be a longer journey but safer.”

“Yes but we would have to be very careful.”

“Well if we watch the rest of them, including Limpy, you at the back me at the front, we can between us ensure they are safe as they can be.”

“Yes I think that could work, so are we telling them the problems we face?”

“Not at this time but we may need to as we get nearer.”

Jobe took a last look at the map and replaced it in his pocket for safety. They signalled the the group it was time to move on, and Deacon and Jobe lead them off.

The rain had eased a bit though such damp conditions created further issues, with slippery paths along the way. After a while the day was getting old, they had travelled quite away but still remained a long and unfamiliar journey to all of them. It would soon be time to rest for the night and the group were all hungry and rather wet, but the clouds and the rain continued. As they rounded a bend some welcome cover from the weather emerged, which put a smile back on their tired faces.

“Right”, Jobe said, “ Here we will rest for the night, it has been a long trek and we all need to rest and eat. I will go and sort some food out, Arco are you able to join me it will be quicker together.”

“Right you are Jobe,”

Jobe and Arco set off in search of food for the group, Deacon stayed behind with the group to help them settle in.

Jude came up to Deacon for a chat,

"You and Jobe seem to be getting along, are you ok together? It has been a difficult time for you both."

"We get on alright, it is something his father said to him, just after Heti died. I didn't hear but he seemed to listen. I understand there may be tension but time will tell, he seems happy for me to help, and asks for my advice."

"Yes, he does, there is an old saying, bit like my name, in olden days my name meant saint of hopeless cases, but keep you friends close and your enemies closer, so just be careful."

"Yes, I have heard that saying, but I will be careful."

In the distance the silhouette of Jobe and Arco signalled it was time for some food. The day had been long but still the rain continued. As Jobe and Arco laid the food out on the ground, they all had plenty to eat, but the day was old and the night drew ever closer.

"Right, we will rest here for the night," Jobe announced, "we will set off at first light in the morning and continue onward."

Jude asked the question,

"Where are we going Jobe? And how long will it be before we are there?"

"It may be a few days yet, we have the map, and planned a route, we are going in the right direction but as we have to be careful, it may seem long but we will get there, and safely."

"Yes I know, but where are we going?"

"It is a place indicated on the map, called 'The Longshoot', it lies on a hill so we can see all the way round. One side is steep and rocky, the other slightly easier and has all we need, it is well away from the humans but we are able to keep an eye on the surroundings. I can see no human paths indicated in the area, but this is an old map so we will know more when we get there."

"I don't like the sound of longshoot," Limpy commented, "it reminds me of the humans and their smoking guns, are you sure we will be safe!"

"We will see Limpy don't worry yet."

They all finished their food and the night was upon them, it was time to settle down for the well earned sleep, make ready for the day ahead. Deacon sat beside Jobe,

"Jobe, what you said, why did you not mention the human village or the swamp?"

"Deacon, you heard Jude, they are scared and to add the possibility of human contact or the swamp, do you think they would still come with us?"

"Yes but if they find out, then we may lose confidence in us,"

"Possibly but we will have to see, we may have to tell them, but nearer the time. You also need to trust me."

"I do, but not telling them everything, it reminds me of, you know."

"We are fine, and if we have to tell them, we will."

With that, they both settled for the night. As Deacon drifted off to sleep, Jobe sat and looked out across the forest and said a silent prayer for his Mother. He looked up to the sky as a shooting star wizzed across the clearing sky, this was followed by a wish.

—— **Chapter 2** ——

A Worrying Encounter

Jobe woke following a restless night, the conversations of last night with Deacon played heavy on his mind. He recalled the deception Deacon was forced to endure, but he was encouraged that it was now all out in the open. The clouds had dispersed to a point, and some break in the weather was of great relief. It was to be a pleasurable journey as nobody really enjoyed the rain, but it would be another long tiresome day.

"Ok everyone, make sure that you have all you need, clear away anything that may encourage the humans to follow."

"Are we close to humans then Jobe? I thought we were keeping our distance?" Jude replied.

"There is a slight chance of human contact, but only a slight one, this is new territory for all of us, although the map shows us a route, it is old, and things change. So we have to be careful and aware, but stick together we should be fine."

"Oh, let's hope we don't meet humans." Jude said nervously.

"Where possible, we will keep away from humans, but at times, we may be close."

Deacon spoke,

"We know where we want to be, but in order to get there we need to pass by Summercoats, a human village. If we are quiet, Limpy are you listening, we shouldn't have any issues."

"Come on, we must get on, while the weather is ok."

They all set off following Jobe and Deacon, Jude continued bringing up the rear, making sure that there was no trail to follow, marking every turn. Another sharp shower dampened the journey, Jude had a little moan about all the walking. Some human path markings began to emerge as they followed towards Testament river. Just the thought of crossing it was a daunting task, as Jobe recalled his last encounter with the beast from the deep, and his untimely swim earlier in the year.

Jude was a little apprehensive as the human pathways became more frequent.

"Jobe, are you sure we should be this close to the humans, look there are signs everywhere."

"Jude, you will see these things, but not everywhere will the humans be, just a chance. If we keep to the side of the paths we can still hide if anyone comes close. Come on, we need to move quicker, stopping and worrying about things that may or may not happen will cause more uncertainty and more likelihood of encountering the humans."

With that the conversation dried up and the group began to more quicker than normal, as the likelihood of the humans became possible.

Jobe signalled to stop, as in the near distance lay a structure, a human structure, that spanned the width of the river. He hadn't seen such a structure for well, ever, he called Deacon over.

"What do you think that is? Obviously human, but what is it?"

They both studied the map, in order to locate where they were and determine what the structure was. They both glanced at map, to pinpoint where they were. In the left hand corner were the signs for the map, the key to what things were.

"Are, that is a bridge, a structure constructed by humans to cross the river." Deacon said.

"It looks a bit unstable though, very old, look the ropes are fraying."

They both told the group to remain here why they took a closer look at the bridge. Slowly they edged closer to the bridge checking there was no humans nearby, it gently swayed in the slight breeze which was ever present and increasing.

"It looks safe enough, but not sure it will take all of us at the same time, look in the middle, some boards are broken."

"One good thing, it looks as though no humans have been here in awhile, a relic from the past maybe. We could use it to cross the river, and then follow it down through the wooded copse, and towards the swamp, then we wouldn't be so close to the village. The village lies just over there, and a bit closer than I thought."

"We would need to be careful crossing it, remember your last swim,"

"How did you hear about that? Jude been telling tales."

"Well maybe a few, you would need to be careful, as you are heavier than the rest of us, no offence"

"None Taken."

With that they returned to the group to report on their findings, and tell them the where they are heading.

"We looked at the bridge structure, it is a bit rickerty, but we should be fine to cross the river as long as it is one by one, then we will travel downstream towards the copse, moving away from the humans."

"Jobe" Limpy said, " are you sure it is not some trap created by the humans? Like the crocodile traps back at the clearing."

"Limpy, humans possibly use it or did, to cross the river, so I don't think it is a trap."

There was a snigger from the group, and Limpy bowed his head and went silent.

"Limpy, you were right to bring it up but we will check it as we get nearer, we will be careful."

It was all Limpy wanted, some recognition from Jobe and Deacon, he mostly just followed them without question. Jobe Turned to Deacon and winked.

They all followed Jobe and Deacon to the bridge, as they arrived the wind was picking up a bit which was a problem. The rain was beginning once more so this added to the issues they faced to cross the river, it would be a challenge for the group who are unfamiliar with structures and the need to cross the river.

The first to cross was Deacon, he volunteered to cross first and mark the unstable boards of the bridge. Once across the others followed one by one, some more frightened than other to cross the bridge. Limpy was the next to cross he was very apprehensive at the prospect and took tentative steps across the structure. The bridge rocked slightly as he edged across the bridge. Half way across a gust of wind took the bridge fiercely, he called out as it shook.

"It's a trap, it's a trap, they are coming to take me away."

Jobe called to him to calm down,

"It is only the wind, and no humans are coming to take you away."

Limpy edged ever closer to the other side, where jude was ready to grab him and help him the last few steps to the other side.

Jobe was the only one left to cross, while the others waited, Jobe began to traverse the bridge. The wind still rocked the bridge, but Jobe's weight steadied it somewhat. Three parts of the way across he trod on what seemed a solid board, his weight suddenly snapped the board in half, his leg slipped through the hole followed by another board breaking and the other leg slipped through. He dug his claws into the boards and tried to haul himself up.

"The humans have got Jobe, help him, help him" Limpy cried.

He was too far away from the group to help him, the group feared for Jobe as he struggled to pull himself up through the boards with his paws.

"Jobe you can do it, you can do it, we need you to pull harder." they all shouted.

Jobe was determined not to fall in the water, no telling how the deep monster would gobble him up. He swung his legs back and forth, the bridge creaked, the group held their breath. Jobe gave one last pull and he was back on the bridge, in relative safety. He wasted no time in covering the rest of the bridge and was safe on the other side. They all gathered round to hug Jobe, thankfully they wouldn't have to call on scar again, something nobody wanted.

"Are you ok Jobe?" Deacon asked.

"I will be fine, once I get my breath back!"

"Has the bridge took your breath, how will you survive?" Limpy asked

"Oh Limpy, it is a figure of speech."

"Right, I knew that, just asking."

"That was unexpected, glad you got back ok." Deacon said.

"I was not looking forward to another swim, but we have to carry on. I guess we will have more to worry about as we near the swamp, and beyond." Jobe replied.

"Don't you think we should tell the group now, as that is where we are heading?"

"Not yet, we will leave it a little longer, look at Limpy, what do you think he will do if we tell them? We need to prepare though and then we will see."

They all set off along the banks of the river testament towards the wooded copse, which would give them some much needed cover. They slowed the pace down now that shade and cover were plentiful, Limpy began to return to his usual self as they continued through the copse.

Up ahead, quite a long way, protruded the peak of Crowsbrook Crag, it was a steep sided hill, that ran down to the river, on the opposite side lay Badgers Fall. The name was a remnant of a past generation, possible as far back as a century of seasons, Jude pointed out the history of it to the group.

"Over there, is Badgers Fall, a steep sided hill, not unlike Crowsbrook Crag, which is there. I only know about it because my great aunty used to tell stories at every get together. Many years ago, there was a wise, a very wise badger who lived up there, on the hillside. After a very wet spring he was returning to his sett, when the whole mountain, well hill moved. They say it was a landslide and he was caught off guard and it swept him down the hill and over the edge of the hill, never to be seen again. He was buried alive beneath tons of soil and rocks, they say at night, those who hear him call out, they will also fall over the edge. Well that is what aunty used to say anyway."

"Do you think we will hear him tonight?" asked Limpy.

"I wouldn't have thought so, it on the other side of the river, I was only telling you the story."

"Good I don't want to swept off the hill, and buried!"

"What hill? Limpy, what hill?"

"Oh Yes, I see."

A rustling up ahead stopped the group in their tracks. They all hid in the bushes and behind trees, as they all feared the humans.

In the distance a strange looking figure walked along the banks of the river. Behind him he pulled a strange looking pointy structure, all the group feared it was a weapon. None dare move for fear of being heard, the hooded figure stopped briefly, before moving on, he looked across at the river. As he neared the group, Jobe was just about to growl when Deacon ushered him to be quiet. He looked round, pulled the structure to the water, calmly got in and floated away down river.

"What was that," Came a chorus of questions.

"I have seen picture of that, they are humans and they use a boat to challenge themselves down rivers, they paddle them and see how far they can travel." Jude had answered the questions.

"Few, good job they didn't see us."

"Don't worry so much, alone and without a weapon we could have taken him on and won."

"I told you the humans have traps, look at the bridge!" Limpy said.

"Guess that was the first of many as we trek across to our new home, we will just have to be careful, stick together so we have a good chance to get to the Longshoot, as a group." Jobe said and continued to walk along the riverbank.

"We are sticking together, who has the glue, who has the glue." Limpy sung.

"Back to normal then are we?"

Limpy just screwed his face up and carried on.

They continued along the river as the day was getting old, the sun had been obscured by the steep sided edges of both Badgers Fall and Crowsbrook Crag. The trees thinned out a little as they walked through the copse, this signalled the copse coming to an end, which could be and issue. Jobe worried that if they carried on any further they could be compromised with lack of cover for the group.

Jobe halted the group, to check the map, both Deacon and Jobe decided that although it was early evening, it would be best to remain here in cover near to the edge of the copse for the night, just to be safe. They all helped to screen the group off as Jobe and Deacon went to source food for the group. Jude stayed with the group to settle them for the night.

"Jude" Limpy said. "What if we hear the badger, will we be swallowed up and buried alive?"

"There will be noises that are unfamiliar to us all, this is new to us, but together, we as a group, will be fine. Jobe is a good leader, Deacon too, so don't worry."

Jobe and Deacon returned back with food and drink for the group, they had travelled many miles, with many more to come. They eat the food and drank the water, settling down for the night. The wind whistled through the valley, and the night took the eyes of them all.

—— **Chapter 3** ——

Familiar Friends

They all woke to a sun filled early morning, feeling more relaxed as their journey beconned. Jobe and Jude went to get some food, as they had yet another long and tiresome journey ahead. Deacon watched over the group as Jobe was away, he contemplated telling them about the swamp, though this would, infuriate Jobe. Both Jobe and Jude returned with a plentiful supply of food, suitable for everyone, there was some fish and plants that are wholesome and full of energy. It was still early but between the clouds shafts of sunlight lit the peak of Crowsbrook Crag and illuminated the direction they were to follow.

"Did you hear the badger last night? I'm sure it was him." Limpy said nervously.

"That was the wind, it whipped through the valley, besides, if that was the case, wouldn't we have been swallowed up." Jude replied.

"Enough of this chat, there are reasonable answers to most things you hear, ghosts and ghouls are a figment of imagination and consist of natural things in the countryside." Jobe said.

Limpy screwed up his face at Jobe, and they quickly finished their food, before moving on.

"Deacon, make sure we leave nothing behind, no trace, before we leave, we know humans are about but less chance that can follow us. Jude, come up front with me?"

They all followed the request, but Jude was worried that Jobe was angry with her, due to the tales she has been telling whilst on the journey.

"Jude," Jobe said, "It seems your aunt was quite knowledgeable about these parts, how is that?"

"She had family round these parts, many years ago, but they knew about this area. That village back there, was close to her family. Something happened between them, but we never found out what. Why?"

"What lies ahead for us then?"

Jobe was trying to find out how much she knew, and if she had an incline about the swamp.

"There are many open spaces, but only from the map, so we need to be careful beyond Crowsbrook Crag. I think there is a weir, which is human built but for what purpose I don't know. It is a rocky structure in the water, beyond that, they never mentioned anything, so we need to be careful."

"I know from the map, we have to go through the long narrow passage so we would need to do this early and not at night, the river runs through the passage between Crowsbrook Crag and Badgers fall, they almost meet in the middle, so we may be vulnerable."

"Yes I know but we have no choice I saw on the map it would take ages to go round, which will be too much for some of us."

"Can I ask that we don't tell any stories, well facts about the upcoming places, including the narrow passage?"

"Yes of course, though there is a tale associated with it."

"Let's keep it quiet till we pass through it, then it will be ok."

"You're not mad at me are you?"

"No, not at all, but look at Limpy, he is a bit of a scatty at times and it could impact on the rest of the group."

"Ok, I see, I will be quiet then."

"Good, so are we ok?"

"Fine."

With those final words, Jobe and Jude Continued to lead the group, Limpy was almost back to normal, which was an issue for Deacon, as he had to keep telling him to be quiet.

The edge of the copse loomed, the trees thinned, as the group ventured into a clearing. The few remaining trees were little cover for the group, so they needed to be careful.

Jobe thought back to the time when he ran after Limpy and ended in a clearing, where crocodile traps were set, also that Foxy was saved. He slowed down the pace to ensure that none were present in this clearing.

"Why so cautious here?" Jude asked.

"Well when Limpy and I went through a clearing months ago, there were traps installed by the humans, one had trapped a fox, but I released it, don't trust a fox! So we just need to be careful."

"So you think there are humans about then?"

"No, not really, but this is new and we don't want anyone getting hurt."

Jude then took to looking for traps as well as Jobe, the long grass was a problem, but soon it became evident they were safe.

A rushing of water signalled the weir was close by, it would be interesting to see the weir, the structure and try to figure out what the purpose of it was. He signalled the group to follow him so that they all could see the weir.

"Right," Jobe announced "We are approaching the weir, as we are in a new area we need to familiarise ourselves with what lay in the area. This on the map is the weir, a structure created by humans to what end I have no idea, but at least we know what it is and where we are in relation to the map."

Jobe lead them all to edge of the water. They all looked at the structure, it was a strange thing seemingly shallow but on either side it was deeper.

"Just to be certain, this is a human structure, but it has been here many years, not sure what it does, or the purpose is, something to do with flow of the river, a bit like a dam. We need to know what is around the area, although quite a way from the Longshoot but in the new area. Just be careful, though it will be deep water either side of the weir, not a place to bathe."

"So why are we here Jobe?"

"I want you to see new things, possible human made but this is learning new things. As we near the Longshoot, we will see new things and these are things to help us determine the surrounding area and make sure we can find our way back, should we lose our way."

"So why would this be important? If we are a long way off."

"As a whole, not really, but just so you know, what it is and where."

Limpy glanced into the deep water, he stepped back, a worrying look on his face.

"What's up with you Limpy?" Jude asked

He didn't want to alarm anyone, so;

"I thought I saw something in the water, but it's gone now."

"You are seeing things." Jude replied.

He was sure something was moving , but they couldn't see anything.

"Right come on, we need to get on."

They all followed Jobe away from the river, Limpy spared a worrying glance back at the river, then moved to the middle of the group.

It was near midday and time for the group rest a little, away from the weir a few more trees had emerged, so an ideal place to rest for a short time. Jobe and Jude went to get some food for the group, and Deacon went to see Limpy.

"So what startled you at the weir?"

"Don't know what you are on about," then looked shifty.

"Come on, you were at the back then moved to the middle, you only do that when something scares you! I can tell Jobe you know."

"No, no, alright; I was looking in the deep water and I saw a shape in the reeds, well green stuff. I didn't want to scare anyone, but it was moving."

"Ok, well that is behind us now, but it could have been debris from further up the river, it had been there a long while. Let's not tell Jobe though."

"Fine by me, but it did move!"

"The current of the water would make it move."

Jobe and Jude returned with berries and mushrooms for the group, and something to drink, whilst the group eat, Jobe took himself away from the group to study the map. He was plotting the next leg of the journey, they would follow the river to Testiment pool and settle there for the night, before attempting the swamp.

Jobe noticed some shrubbery by the pool and decided that this would be the best place for the night, but they would need to move quicker to get there. The group had rested and eaten as Jobe announced the next faze of the journey, and where they would stay for the night.

"Right we have a long journey towards Testament Pool, by the side of the pool there is some shrubbery, which will be good cover for the night. I know it seems that we have been travelling for so long, but we knew it wouldn't be easy. We need to pick up the pace in order to get to Testiment Pool but we have to travel across some open ground, so speed is needed. Come on then let's tidy away and get moving." Jobe said, "Oh Deacon, can you come up front with me now, Jude keep them at the back moving.

They set off at a quicker pace than before, knowing that every minute out in the open, is less safe. Limpy had taken up in the middle again, still unsure of what he did or didn't see in the deep water. Before long the outline of the pool came into view, this promised some well deserved cover and a chance to relax. It had been a nervous few hours but the quicker pace had took the energy out of some of the group. It would become more stressful as they had many more trials before the new homestead was realised. Limpy had almost forgotten about the shape in the river by the weir and was getting back to how used to be.

"Right", Jobe said "I will be settling the group in for the night, we need to shield ourselves from any prying eyes and make sure we have plenty of cover for the night. Can two of you go and find some food and water for us all,"

Limpy was the first to volunteer to go and Deacon agreed to help him, unaware of what had happened earlier in the day.

They both went to the pool for water, there was also an abundance of watercress that greeted their greedy eyes. They both began to harvest the watercress, then suddenly , Limpy saw the shape in the water, he just turned and ran back to the camp, Deacon was stunned and couldn't understand why he had ran.

"We're being attacked, we're being attacked he shouted."

Deacon followed him back, with the food and asked what all the fuss was about.

"I saw a shape in the water, one like at the weir, it tried to pull me in, right in."

Jobe came over to see what all the noise was about.

"Limpy calm down, what is the matter?"

"Back there in the weir, I saw something moving, in the water, I didn't want to scare anyone so didn't say anything, but just then in the pool I saw another shape and it tried to pull me in."

"Deacon, what happened?"

"Jobe I don't know, I never saw anything, Limpy just ran back and shouted something."

"Well," Jude said, " Limpy did tell me about a shape in the water, but I put it down to dedis in the water, as I didn't see it move, by the weir."

"You should have said something, come on let's go and see what all the fuss is about."

Jobe walked to the pool, he was cautious about what may be there, though not unduly bothered. He got to the pool, and looked into the pool, but nothing was visible. Rustling in the reeds startled him and let out a warning growl.

The group heard the growl and Jude went to see what it was all about.

"Told you they are coming to get us there coming to get us."Limpy shouted.

Back at the pool Jobe was just about to let out another warning growl, when a familiar face popped out of the reeds.

"That is a fine way to treat friends Jobe, What are you like."

"Bonso, where have you been?"

"Well after the fire we got seperated , I just found the water and well here I am."

Just then Jude came running towards them,

"Leave him alone!" before realising who it was.

"Fine way to treat friends, Jobe what have you created?"

"Bonso, where have you been?" Jude asked

"I was just telling Jobe, during the fire I just found water, and funny how you're all here, and so territorial."

"Let's have a laugh, I think we need one, but we shouldn't."

Jobe covered Bonso in watercress, and headed back to the camp.

The sun was almost setting as Jobe and Jude returned from the pool. Deacon and Limpy were just about run to the pool when they noticed Jobe and Jude walking back to camp, hands on head.

"The beast from the pool has got Jude and Jobe, we are all finished, hear me finished." Limpy said nervously.

They all feared the worse, their leader and co-leader taken by the beast from the deep.

It was only when Deacon noticed something familiar , a flattened tail, and webbed claws.

"Bonso, you're back."

They all burst out laughing as the friends reunited, after a long while not knowing. Then the party started, the whole group back together.

It was a fun night and far more relaxed than previous nights. There was still a long way to go before they reached their new home, the Longshoot, but now with all the friends back together they could look forward to a new life.

Chapter 4

Swamped

The morning broke with shafts of light illuminating their new home, but many days still remain till they can start their new beginning. They were entering dangerous territory as they aim to cross the swamp, but many dangers lies ahead and although as a group they are strong, it was worrying for Jobe as he lead them towards a new beginning.

"Bonso" Jobe called, "Can I have a word?"

"Yes Jobe, what is it?"

"Not here."

They took a walk together on a quest for food.

"Right, I know you have only just arrived back with us, but we have a challenging journey today."

Jobe retrieved the map and showed Bonso the next leg of the journey, through the swamp.

"We are going round the edge of the swamp, but this is an old map I am unsure if the swamp has increased, since this was produced. You have a specially designed tail and webbed claws, so it would be a help if you could guide us."

"Not as easy as you think, I have heard that the swamp gobbles up a full size horse or cattle. They call it quicksand, and even I wouldn't survive if I landed in it."

"Oh I thought it was only water based swamp,"

"Most of it is, but quicksand is dangerous! What do the rest of them think?"

"That's an issue, I haven't told them yet, I was going to later on before we leave."

"You need to tell them Jobe, you know as well as I what happens when you keep secrets, they need to understand the dangers."

" I agree, but will you still help us?"

"Yes Jobe, but be clear if you fall in the quicksand you won't get out."

"Ok, we will tell the group, but I think we may have a problem on our hands."

Jobe and Bonso returned to the group, with food and supplies, Deacon and Jude directed the group.

"Gather round everyone;" Jobe announced, "Right we are at a critical part of the journey, the next stage is to bypass the swamp. Now there are some downsides to this part, Bonson has informed me that there is some quicksand. This is nasty stuff, so we need to be calm, collected and methodical. Bonso will be up front with me, Deacon, will take the centre, and Jude bring up the rear. Limpy, this is no time for silly games, it is dangerous and you need to understand that. Both me and Boson will have sticks with us, this is to prod the ground in front of us. Make no mistake, do not deviate from the path we tread."

"Is there another way, it seems dangerous."

"There is another route, but this would mean several more days of travel and another village to pass, there we will no doubt see humans, so not really."

"I don't like it, I don't like it at all, at least with humans we can see them and hide."

"Remember the clearing, we struggled to see the crocodile traps, and I am unsure if there will be much cover."

"Point taken, the sooner we get the the Longshoot the better."

"Let's go for it, I trust you and now Bonso."

"Good let's get on, I want to be out of the swamp before nightfall."

Jobe and Bonso headed off along the stream, the rest of the group followed close behind. They set off along the stream towards Ruffcoat hill, the stream, lay to the right of them to guide them forward. It was easy going at first, as the swamp was quite away ahead but this would be a treacherous journey for all of them.

"Bonso, thanks for this, it will save us time ." Jobe said.

"Let's hope we don't regret it , we have seen so much tragedy these last few months."

"I know all too well but we have to look forward and not dwell on the past."

The journey was slow, nobody really wanted to reach the swamp, as the ground became less supportive of Jobe he signalled the beginning of the swamp.

Both Jobe and Bonson began the endless testing of the the ground in front of them, this to ensure it was safe to travel over it. At times it was very muddy, Jobe was cautious, as he was the heaviest of all of them. Bonso was ok as he had webbed claws but he was suited to the water but he was buoyant. It was tedious to say the least, but due to how serious the quicksand could be they couldn't risk any mistakes.

Just then Jobe's stick slipped deep into the ground, he drew the group to a halt:

"We need to be careful here." and he marked the area. Jobe drew the stick out and tested the ground all round him, one side was solid the other was quicksand, it was like a trap ready to engulf them. Bonso directed him to where his paws needed to be placed, they slowly edged round the quicksand. Each one of the group followed where they were to tread. Soon it was Limpy's turn, he was so nervous.

"The quicksand's going to get me, don't let it get me!"

"Calm down Limpy everyone is with you, we will watch out for you. Listen to what we are telling you, follow the instructions. One of his feet slipped into the quicksand, then it began to pull him in, further and further.

Jobe was quickest to react, and he grabbed him and pulled him free from the quicksand.

"You're ok Limpy, we've got you."

Once on solid ground he moaned that the sandman tried to get him.

"I don't like this." Bonso said.

"Neither do I, but we will soon be out of the swamp, there may be other pockets close by so we need to be careful as we go forward." Jobe said and carried on.

The group were so careful it was taking a long time to travel but a short distance, Bonso and Jobe were taking more time to examine the ground in front of them.

"Jobe." Bonso said, "It seems to be getting damper this way, maybe we should go further round."

"What's to say it gets worse further round, at least this way we are covering some ground, these damp conditions are not good for the group. The sooner we get out the better."

Jobe was too interested in getting out he didn't check the ground immediately in front of him. Suddenly his left leg began to sink, the more he pulled the deeper it sank.

"Stop." shouted Bonso. "Jobe is stuck in quicksand."

Jobe Panicked as he tried to release his leg, each time it sank deeper, Bonso called to Jude and Deacon to come and help, this was dangerous.

"Stay here, all of you, and don't move." Deacon went to assist.

He followed the line that they had already taken and headed to where Jobe was stranded.

"Jobe, listen to me," Jude said, "The more you struggle the deeper you will sink."

"That's easy for you to say, your not sinking."

"Listen, my aunty used to say, if you ever get stuck in quicksand, relax, and don't struggle. It will take a while, but you need to slowly pull your leg out, only a bit at a time. Bonso, lay your staff across the solid part of the ground. Jobe lean over it when you pull, then relax, do this a bit at a time, don't struggle."

"The sandman's got Jobe, the sandman's got Jobe." Limpy shouted.

"Limpy, will you shut up, you're not helping, Jobe will be fine, but it will take a little time to release him. Right lean on the staff, and pull, slowly now. Rest, now lean and pull, slowly now."

Jude kept on with the chatter for what seemed like ages. Little by little, Jobe's leg came out of the quicksand, until finally he was free, and he breathed a sigh of relief and caught his breath.

The whole group were quiet, even Limpy didn't say another word. After a while Jobe was ready to move on, they marked the quicksand, Jude and Deacon moved back to their positions. Time was getting on, Jobe and Bonso ensured every step was on solid ground, till they reached the edge of the swamp, now lay a wide open space to quickly get across before nightfall.

"Right, we are safely out of the swamp, but we need to move quickly towards those trees, open spaces are not great, but we need to get to the trees before we rest." Jobe said.

Their pace quickened across the open space, Limpy still quiet, followed and Jude Pushed the rest to keep up the pace. Soon they reached the edge of the trees which lay in the shadow of Roughcoat.

Roughcoat was a steep sided hill, but unstable, there were indications of recent landslides. The rocky outlook was visible, the base was lined with trees, some as old as the world, rocks as big as houses littered the face. The clouds had gathered round the top of Roughcoat, the threat of rain was imminent, something that had been absent for a few days. The group set up camp on the outskirts of the forest, just far enough in to be safe and covered, the whole group was worn out and after the issues of the day, due a rest.

"Ok, we set up camp here, as we are unsure of what lies ahead in the forest, there does not seem to be a visible path so best we rest. While we are getting some food, Jude and Deacon can you help secure the area and best we sort out a canopy as rain will soon be upon us. Thanks."

While Jobe and Bonso went for food Jude and Deacon set up a canopy to protect them from rain, they all went to clean the mud off by the stream, they all stuck together as none were sure of what lies ahead and as a group they are safer.

When they returned everyone was cleaner and the camp was set up for the night, it would be a long night, as they were all tired.

Jobe and Deacon went to check the map and have a look for any signs of a path. There was a need to mark the map from now on as there was little indication of paths and other information leading to the Longshoot. It seemed that the map was not updated and things may have changed in the years long past. It was decided to update the map at every stop and along the way if required. Once these updates were done a new map can be drawn up to assist the group and others once they reach the Longshoot. They both returned to camp in order to settle down the group for the night. A rubble of thunder in the distance signalled a storm would be upon them, nobody liked a storm, not even Jobe.

The night descended on the camp and everyone settled down for a well earned sleep, tomorrow would bring new challenges, that as a group they will need to overcome.

—— Chapter 5 ——

Recollection 'A Nightmare'

Jobe tossed and turned as the thunder echoed in the distance, his mind full of memories from the early part of the year. So much had happened in such a short time, his bearcub days stripped of enjoyment. Trauma had been suppressed, hidden, in his quest for survival following the death of his mother. Scar, his absent father, roamed the mountains, alone, hidden away from the human interest in his death. Jobe was now alone, young, inexperienced in the ways of life, which as a family they should have learnt together.

Flashes of lightning flickered in the distance, reviving memories of the red mist, the fire that chased the whole kingdom away. Red hot flames licked the tree before igniting them and shattering the aged branches of the trees. Jobe called out to his friends to run, the red mist was coming. His mother sauntered towards him, the flames licking her fur, she cried out but Jobe couldn't hear her call, scared of the red hot whiskers of the red mist.

Jobe heard his father's growl, a warning, the exploding trees like gunfire, his father ran and ran, but the humans were gaining on him, closer, closer they came, Scar cried out in pain, as the red hot bullet sliced through his fur.

From the water emerged Wenlock, this ever present beaver struggled out of the boiling water, his skin red and blistered, the river ran with death on its surface, fish, scallops, and frogs floating aimlessly in the boiling hot water. Wenlocks dam burnt like a fire, and the greedy red mist consumed the wooden structure , feeding greedily on the dead as they floated by.

Foxy chased Limpy unaware of the crocodiles that lay in the clearing, as each one snapped at his legs, he cried out in pain as the hungry crocodiles nibbled his legs. The red mist happy to feast on the body of foxy, unable to move, he was devoured. In the distance a lop sided stag jumped, his head to one side since the humans took his soul. Bentner was the all conquering stag, though humans assisted him in times of need, he would be killed given the chance the humans thirst for blood unwavering. Suddenly he fell to the ground, a cry of pain indicated he had succumbed to the human chase, the red hot blade of the humans tools sliced through the antler in order to line their own pockets. The red mist chased away the humans, its red hot tongue licked the body of Bentner and his last cry echoed. Breezedon tried to chace the red mist away to save Bentner, but the red hot hands of the red mist grabbed his sturdy body and Breezedon cried as the red mist quench its thirst for death.

Jobe Woke with a start, as Jude shook him,

"Jobe are you ok, Jobe, Jobe."

Jobe roused slightly from his sleep,

"What's up, what's happening, the red mist, where is it now?"

Jude and Bonso looked at each other,

"Jobe, the red mist has gone, we left it behind, besides it is still dark, you woke us up."

"Oh, really. You have just woken me up."

"No panic Jobe, sorry, you were dreaming."

"Dreaming, I was fast asleep, now let me sleep we have another long day ahead of us tomorrow."

Both Jude and Bonso left him to sleep as the sound of thunder seemed ever closer.

"What do you make of that Jude?"

"Not sure, we will need to keep an eye on him, he seems to be having flashbacks from the fire."

"A flashback, what is one of those?" Bonso added.

"It is a vivid recollection of things that have happened, memories, nightmares."

"I have heard of nightmares, at times Limpy is a nightmare."

"I heard that, " Came a voice from the next tree.

"Sorry Limpy, didn't mean to wake you."

"Wake me, Jobe woke me, and this thunder. I don't like thunder."

They all settled back to sleep as the storm rolled in.

Jobe drifted off to sleep again, unsure why he was woken up by Jude. The thunder rolled in and the lightning flashed as Jobe descended back to sleep.

The red mist curled in the wind, its fiery arms lashed out at unsuspecting trees, singeing the fingers of their newly formed leaves. Unaware of the red mist Herronetty bathed in the pond as the red mist lit up the heads of the reeds, singeing her feathers as she bathed. The realisation of the fire raged all around her, she immediately took flight, but the extending hands of the red mist grabbed her body dragging her back into the mouth of the ever hungry fire. Thrifty watched in dismay, as the fire engulfed all in its path, no way could she outrun the flames that kill and boil all that's dear to her. The relentless heat and smoke burnt her chest and singed her nostrils. The poisonous smoke overtook her body and she sank to the ground without a sound.

Jobe Sniveled as the nightmare continued, a single tear slipped from his eye.

All those he knew slipped from his thoughts, engulfed in the fire and consumed. A rapture of thunder echoed overhead which woke jobe from his sleep.

"They are all gone, all gone." Tears welled in his eyes, Jude and Bonson heard his call and went to see what all the fuss was about.

"Jobe what's up?" Bonso asked.

"They are all gone!"

"Who's gone, where have they gone?"

Jobe was still not fully awake , Jude and Bonso looked at each other, not sure quite what to do.

"Jobe wake up, Jobe." They shouted.

Suddenly he was fully aware of where he was, and his friends were there too.

"What's up?" he asked

"Jobe, do you not remember?"

"Remember what! I have been asleep, I see the storm is brewing!"

"You shouted, everyone's gone!" Jude replied.

"Jobe, who's gone?" Bonso asked.

Jobe shook his head, still unclear he had been dreaming, none the wiser for his outburst, either. Jude and Bonso went back to the tree they came from.

"What do you make of that?" Jude asked

"Beats me, it must have been a nightmare, he is young and quite a lot has happened to the little fellow."

"What do we do?"

"I would leave it, he can't remember what has just happened, it was a dream, I have had a few of them myself these last few weeks."

"Yes, me too, we just carry on , sort our own demons out."

"Demons, where, I don't like demons." Limpy said.

"It is just a figure of speech Limpy, that's all."

"Good, don't want demons in the new place."

Jobe called Jude over,

"Can you come with me and we can sort out some food before we leave, though no fish today, the stream is too small."

"Yes Jobe, come let's see what we can find."

They both went off to sort some food out, water was available from the small stream. Deacon and Bonso got together to help pack things away but the thunder rattled and seemed somewhat closer. The clouds were billowing up as Jobe and Jude returned, the showers had become more of a torrent, and the constant thunder indicated the closeness of the storm. They sat down for food before making their way towards the Longshoot.

The vegetation was thick, which made it difficult and at a slower pace than normal, at times the bushes clawed at the travellers. The rain and thunder became more apparent, the lightning was forceful and worrying to the group, there was an increased risk of a strike on the trees. A ferocious clap of thunder indicated a lightning strike in the distance, an aged tree exploded. Jobe stopped, in fright, recalling some of the trees as the red mist took hold in the forest. He was worried that they would be confronted by fire..

"I think we need to stop, this storm is starting to take hold. I don't want risk injury so we make camp now." Jobe announced.

Jude looked around, there was the face of Roughcoat which was sheer and could be dangerous.

"Do you think we should move away from the side of the hill, it looks rocky and risky so close."

Jobe looked round, and agreed to a point so they moved inward into the forest but in the area of Roughcoat. There was some taller trees but rocks can be an issue if dislodged.

"I see what you mean so if we move in the forest a bit we are going to be safer, but not too far. Maybe just the other side of the stream it is not deep."

They crossed the stream and set up camp as the storm took hold. They all huddled together beneath the canopy of branches to wait the storm out. Lightning and thunder echoed, the day would be long.

Chapter 6

The Storm

Jobe looked worried, a violent storm on the horizon was building, not just one but three. The fact that at this time three storms encroached their position it was dangerous but they could do little about it. The thunder raptured almost constantly as the storms brewed, the rain was the heaviest he had ever seen, in his short life. He decided that the colony would need to remain here for the day as the storm didn't seem to be subsiding.

"Jude, Bonso and Deacon," Jobe called them all over. "This storm will be massive it seems we have three coming together, you could say the perfect storm, but not for us. We need to prepare for some serious rain and we need a canopy that will cover all of us together, we have not a lot of time so we need to be quick."

All three of them went out to collect shrubbery for the canopy and Jobe ensured the canopy was secured as the wind was starting to blow. Soon all the shrubbery was gathered and the canopy built, it was the best they could do in the time available.

The lightning flashed as the whole sky seemed to be alive with electrical current, first sheet lightning traversed the sky, followed by the rumbles of thunder. Then from nowhere fork lightning flashed and as it shattered an aged tree in the distance, a clap of thunder, louder than any of the group had heard echoed. Fork lightning is the most dangerous of all, its sheer power able to set fire to trees and explode anything it chooses, the memories of the red mist still apparent in everyone's thoughts. The rain pelted down on the canopy and streams of water emerged down the side of Roughcoat swelling the stream below.

"Jobe, I don't like this storm, it seems angry, and we are in the middle of it.." Jude Said

"I'm not keen on it either, the fork lightning is dangerous, look what it did to that tree over there." Jobe pointed.

"Jobe." Bonso said, "We need to keep and eye on the stream, as the rain swells it, to make sure it doesn't flood. If it does we could be in some trouble!"

"I see, what do you think, move?"

"No, we need the shelter, I noticed down stream a few branches were clogging it up, this will hold the water back. I will go downstream and clear the stream so the water can run faster, that would give us a better chance of preventing a flood."

"Ok, you do that and if you need a hand come and get me."

"Right you are Jobe."

With that Bonso slipped into the water and set off in his quest to clear the obstructions downstream. Another strike of lightning downstream indicated how bad the storm was, Jobe hoped that Bonso was ok.

Bonso reached the corner where the stream had turned, he began to remove the branches and sticks from the cluster. It was quite hard work and more sticks floated down, he gnawed through those he could but one was especially thick, a fallen tree lay across the stream. Bonso needed help to remove the tree, and returned to the camp for help. Bonso slipped out of the stream and went to speak with Jobe, he would need help to remove the tree and Jobe was the obvious choice.

Jobe and Bonso returned to the corner where the stream turned, the debris was already building up again and the water was nearing the banks. Realising that the water was increasing it was imperative that the tree was moved as any surge of water would turn to flood.

"Quick, help me with this branch, we need to use a fulcrum, and then let the water take it away."

"What's a fulcrum? " Bonso asked.

"It is something my dad said once, what you do is, get some bits of wood, or branches, place the wood near to the thing you want to move and use another piece of wood, longer than the rest, slide it between the two and ease down, do this bit by bit and you can move big things. We need to do this now, as the water will flood soon."

While Jobe and Bonso worked on the tree, the water had backed up to the camp and Jude was worried.

"Jude, I think we should move, look at the water it will flood soon."

"We can't move how will Jobe find us." Deacon said

"Then we need to build a barrier of rocks to keep the water back, all of us need to do it, we don't have much time." Jude replied.

They all set off to gather rocks. After countless journeys the barrier was built just round the camp but the water was rising.

Jobe and Bonso were struggling to remove the tree.

"We need to get this tree moved the water is backing up, the camp will be flooding soon."

"Easier said than done."

They both struggled with the tree to get it to move, it was slow process but bit by bit the tree was moving, but the water was building.

"That's it we are getting somewhere, we need to move this quickly look at the water!"

At the camp the water was building up and it was lapping the barrier, they all moved back from the barrier beneath the trees. The rain pounded the canopy, a disturbing rumble from the side of Roughcoat troubled

Jude and Deacon. Both looked at each other unsure of what the rumble was, but they couldn't see anything from where they were.

It was Limpy who saw it first, he rubbed his eyes in disbelief, as he thought the hill moved.

"The hill is moving, it's running away, the hill is moving."

"What are you on about Limpy? Hill's don't move, they just don't."

"I'm telling you, the hill is moving."

Jude and Deacon looked puzzled at Limpy.

"What do you think he is on about?" asked Jude

"Search me, hill's don't move!"

A few rocks rolled down the side of the hill, which took their gaze, all of them watched the rocks rolling down.

"I told you the hill moved, look." Limpy said

"Don't be silly Limpy, hills don't move."

"That one does, look."

They all looked up to see the whole side of the hill slip towards the stream, as it gained pace, all of them began to panic. They had little choice but to move upstream, away from the camp, it built up at the side of the stream and then one large boulder rattled down and bounced into the water. This sent a tidal surge upstream and downstream, the camp was wiped out, Jude and Deacon worried that Jobe and Bonso had no idea what was coming.

Jobe heard the rush of water and the rumble, turning sharply, the water was flowing towards them and a massive wave rolled towards them, Jobe was worried.

"We need to push Bonso, quick look at the wave, we need to go."

With one last massive effort the tree was released, Jobe and Bonso moved away as the wave picked up the tree and took it downstream and the build up of water diminished.

"Few that was close, what do you think caused that rush of water?"

"I don't know I just hope the camp is ok, that was a lot of water."

It was only then it hit him, what about the camp the others in the group, they were all alone. They both headed back to the camp, as they neared it was evident something catastrophic had happened and the camp was gone, nothing left of it, it was totally submerged. The landslip had all but covered the camp, the stream was blocked and no sign of any life.

Jobe's heart sank, all his friends had gone, lost to the storm, buried. He sat down in sadness, he had failed to protect his colony, and now just the two of them were left. Jode's eyes filled with tears for all his friends, Bonson patted him on the back to comfort his sadness.

Suddenly from deeper in the forest came a familiar voice.

"I told you the hill moved, I told you the hill moved." sang Limpy

"Ok, so you saw the hill move, Oh hi Jobe you done that job then?" Jude said.

Jobe breathed a sigh of relief as the all his friend appeared from in the forest, and they all hugged each other.

"I thought you were all, well you're not." Jobe said.

"Don't worry so much Jobe we can look after each other you know, we saw the danger well Limpy saw it first, and we moved away from it." said Jude

"I am glad you did."

The rain had eased a little, and the thunder clouds had moved away, showers were prominent throughout the rest of the day. They remained in the forest for the day as it was undercover.

"I wasn't expecting that storm, were you?" Jobe asked

"Not that bad, hopefully we can rest today and get moving tomorrow." Jude replied.

"Seems like a plan to me, besides, let some of this rain subside first, we are in uncharted territory now. The map has only brief outlines of what lies in front of us, we will update the map as we go, but we need to be vigilant."

They all settled down, though the rain still poured, but as the breaks in the clouds came the limited sunlight flickered in the forest.

"Today we rest, we are all tired and wet, we can hope for a better day in the morning, so get settled in for the night. You may need new bedding if you can find some that is dry, but get some rest, we are closer to our new home, but there is still a way to go. Now we may encounter new things as we go forth, but if we stick together and communicate we will soon get to our new home." Jobe's announcement was concluded and the camp disbanded and went to collect new bedding for the night ahead.

Jobe and Bonso took themselves away from the camp to update the map and discuss the next stage of the journey.

Jobe indicated where he thought they may encounter problems, they were once again in close proximity to a village, and the tale of a wolf that roamed the countryside was worrying. As the day drew to a close the whole group settled down for a well earned rest.

—— **Chapter 7** ——

The Wolf of Liberty

Just as the dawn was breaking, Jobe was woken by a howl that echoed through the forest. At first he thought the wind was gathering and whistling through the forest. He recalled a tale, one that nobody could confirm, that in some parts of the distant forest, a lone wolf patrolled the open spaces that divided the county. He couldn't recall exactly where the tale came from, or who told him about it, only that there was one.

As the camp began to rouse from a well earned sleep, Jobe explained the next stage of the journey.

"Gather round, all of you; I know we have been travelling for a long time, over there, in the distance is our new home. Soon we will be there, but still we have a long way to travel. The Map has only basic information on it from this point, an outline of the area, so we need to be careful. Once through the forest we have some open spaces to cross, we know how dangerous this can be, there is however some cover, and this will be advantageous to us. Just keep aware of those around you and where you are going, we know little of what to expect so keep your eyes peeled."

With that the camp began to pack up, still ensuring no trace of them being there, for any would be followers. Jude went to see Jobe she was uneasy about something.

"Jobe, did you hear the howling last night?"

"Yes Jude, I did, I thought it was the wind through the trees."

"I didn't want to say anything, but there is a tale associated with this area."

"No doubt your aunty told you."

"No, grandma actually."

"Right, what would this tale be associated with?"

"A wolf that roams these parts."

"I am aware of such a tale, but maybe save it for another day."

"Ok Jobe, just wanted to make you aware of such a tale."

Jude returned to the camp, keeping the tale of the wolf to herself. Jobe wondered if there was any truth in the tale, he thought though, if there was such a wolf that roamed the county, why did his dad not say anything about it.

"Come on then, look sharp, we need to get a move on we have a lot of ground to cover."

The camp, what was left of it, was cleared away. They went through the last remnants of the forest, it was hard going, there was no identified pathway, the bushes and trees encroached there direction of travel.

Jobe up front with Bonso, slashed at the undergrowth to make some kind of path. Jude and Deacon marked each turn and direction to indicate the direction and ensure they did not circle. It was long and hard work for all of them, no other visible signs of life were about. After a while the trees and the undergrowth thinned out indicating the end of the forest, and nearer to the open ground. As the trees finished Jobe halted the group, the ground was not as overgrown as the forest but it didn't offer cover either.

"Right, this is the edge of the forest, our next challenge is to cross the open ground and get to the copse over there in the distance. Now, we have little cover so we must keep low and close to the hedgeline, then one by one we will cross the open space, remember low and quick. I will follow once you are all safe, I am more visible than the rest of you, so I will go last."

Deacon was the first to go, the rest of the group kept an eye on the surrounding area, just in case. Once he was safely over it was time for the rest to follow one by one. Soon it was Limpy's turn, he was a little hesitant to say the least. Little by little he moved along the hedgeline, all the rest except for Jobe were safely across. Suddenly a flutter of wings startled Limpy, he cowered as an eagle swooped as if to attack him. Jobe let out a roar and startled the eagle, who then took flight.

"Hurry up Limpy, see what happens when you take your time."

"I don't like eagles they feast on us."

"That's as may be, the quicker your here the better."

Limpy made a run for it, and just as he reached the copse, he tripped on a branch and rolled and rolled, till he landed at the base of a tree. The whole group laughed, as Limpy shook his head and his ears lapped his face.

Jobe heard as noise, just before he was due to move, a strange figure appeared from the undergrowth,

"Hello Jobe, I have some news from the forest, as you near the Longshoot, the friends of Sharply Hollow have located a cave for you to reside in. The old bear has moved closer to his family to allow you to set up a new home. Nearby you will have all the things you need and your friends will have all they require. I am here to look after you as you cross the open spaces, and to assist in the setting up of the colony. You have liberated these animals from certain death and you have lost loved ones along the way. Do not be afraid to call on me, if you ever need me, I reside by night in the old barn, I am at your service."

Before Jobe could answer or react the figure disappeared into the undergrowth.

"Jobe, Jobe, come on, what are you waiting for?" shouted Jude.

"I was just, never mind I will be with you soon."

Jobe went to ground, as low as he could get, the hedge was barely covering his sizable frame. He was unsure what had just happened, but did not fear what he had heard.

Jobe arrived at the copse now all the animals were safely across the open ground, he starred back to the forest wondering what had just happened. He was sceptical about the figure in the undergrowth, his mind toying with the possibility that he had just met the Wolf of Liberty.

"What took you so long back there?" Asked Deacon,

"Oh, I was just thinking of all that had happened, now we are near to our new home."

"Right, but we were told to hurry."

"Yes, I am sorry." Jobe replied.

Jobe then took up the lead and the group moved swiftly into the copse, it was quite dense and overgrown with brambles, they tore at the fur of the group. It was a dark and strange copse, Jobe noticed a distinct lack of birdsong, but couldn't quite work out why.

"Deacon, do you think it is strange, in the fact there is no birdsong in this copse?"

"Now you come to mention it, it is quiet! not sure why though!"

"Maybe it's the wolf of Liberty's home, which could account for the quietness." Jude said.

"It's just a myth though, isn't it?" Deacon said.

"Well, I have heard rumours, that it is no myth, but who knows. That would account for many things, including the quietness of the copse, at this time of the day."

"Well we will have to stay alert, and together, whilst we travel through the copse, but would it be safe to stay at night?" Deacon said.

"Safe, yes, I have heard that the Wolf of Liberty resides at night in the the old barn, it is on the outskirts of the village, over there." Pointing across the open fields. "We will not be going anywhere near the village, so we should be ok for the night."

"Who told you Jobe? My grandma never said anything about that."

"Just something dad said last time we met, don't worry, we will soon be at the Longshoot."

They continued through the copse and struggled with the brambles that obstructed their passage. Jobe's mind wondered back to what he had heard back in the forest, he needed further confirmation of what he had heard. As the day grew old the thinning of the vegetation indicated they were nearing the edge of the copse. Though Jobe did worry about the tale, and the lack of birdsong within the copse, he knew they had little choice but spend the night on the edge of the copse.

"Right, although we have all heard the tale, we will need to spend the night on the edge of the copse, there is a small cluster of trees between here and Brindley copse, but not sure how safe we would be there. It is getting late so we camp here, then at first light we can travel across the open space and break at the cluster of trees over there. Jude can you come with me we need food, and the rest can set up the camp.

Jude followed Jobe in search of food and water, it was quite difficult to find all the food they required, but soon they had enough for everyone.

"Jobe, you seem troubled, what is it?"

"It has been a long trip, and this is all new to us, we have travelled many miles, and I guess all the pressure is building up and we near our new home."

"I understand, so it is not the Wolf of Liberty then?"

"Why would you say that?"

"You're not the only one he spoke too, you know."

"What he spoke to you!"

"Only briefly, the other night, but he was ok."

"What did he tell you?"

"The same as he told you I guess, that was what startled you, wasn't it?"

"Well I was not quite sure what it was."

"Don't worry, we are safe." Jude remarked.

"Let's get back, say nothing!"

"Ok."

Jude and Jobe returned to camp with food enough for everyone; Jobe settled the camp down just as the sun was setting, he was troubled yes, but needed proof.

Jobe slipped away from the group just as night time fell, there was a bright moon as he travelled alone across the field towards the barn, the moon lit his way. As he reached the barn he gently tapped on the door.

"Come in Jobe." Came a rough voice from within.

Jobe entered, not knowing what to expect,

"How did you know it was me?"

The wolf pointed at the rafters,

"I knew you were coming, the minute you left the camp, old wise followed you, he has excellent sight in the dark."

"Oh, so he watched over me."

"He's watching over all of you, since you left the swamp, brave move, but stupid, you could have been killed."

"I thought it was the best way."

"Indeed, your father asked me to keep an eye on you, it has been a traumatic time for one so young, you are a brave bear and a good leader."

"I am not sure; we are moving into a new home and I don't know what to expect."

"Expect nothing, be wise, be friendly, be honest and you will be fine. Ben Delly has provided you with a cave, and the rest will work it out as a team."

"Why has, Ben Delly moved out?"

"His long suffering partner passed away, not unlike your mother, he needs to be close to his family now. As he is older than the hills and can't look after himself."

"So I am not forcing him out?"

"No, he knew you were coming this is your destiny now and the whole colony knows what you have been through. You are young, and you will learn, but you will not be alone for long."

"Is dad coming?"

"Sadly not, it is too far, but trust me you have liberated all you friends from the red mist, you will meet new friends. Those friends will play their part in securing the future of the colony. Jobe you had better return they will miss you, some will ask where you have been , don't mention my place of residence. Jude knows and will help you, now let me rest."

With that Jobe left the barn to return to camp, the moon lit his way back, he knew on his return they would be safe, it was quiet but that was what was expected.

He settled for the night, he contemplated on what had been said, and all that would soon come to pass. He was pleased that they were not as lonely as they thought, all the way here, to this point, on the brink of a new life, but assisted without knowledge.

The night took his eyes, and the bright moon shone over the camp, a few more days would bring them to their new home, and time to settle before the winter set in.

Chapter 8

Larette

Larette, ambled through the woods of Sharpley Hollow, the sun was barely visible in the sky. A strange mist hugged the trees as the cold breath of the morning brushed her fur. It was a sure sign that Autumn was closing in, she always likes the Autumn all those wonderful colours as the leaves start to turn, the flowers of summer blooming, though the grass was burnt by the sun. The days were shorter as the year moved on, the summer solstice passing by. She was pleased that her grandfather had moved from his cave at the Longshoot, though all the happy times she spent there were to be lost. She was a lonely bear, no kin but for her family and the friends of the forest she has made along the way. Being the only bear she feared that she could not learn of this world, her grandma passed, it was a sad time, but life seems to continue.

Larette still visited the forest close to the Longshoot, and the remote copse of Brindley, where incidentally she spent many happy times with her grandparents.

As she sauntered through the countryside, her mind wandered to a strange dreams she had been having of late. Some bits she remembered, unfamiliar animals, strange adventures, this recurring dream played heavy on her mind. She had shared the outlines what she remembered with her mother who tried to explain and help her to understand, passing it off as adolescence. Explaining she would be clear in the coming months. She still found it hard to understand and even the friends who had been told could not relay what the dreams meant.

Larette skipped through the trees of Brindley Copse, there her swing, many years old now, it still hung but in disrepair following her grandma's illness, before the passing of his partner, Ben Delly, Larette's Grandad, promised to repair it for her, though he never really got the time. Her Father had not the time to repair the swing either, he was out most days patrolling the Northern quarter of the county. Humans were his nemesis. Humans had taken over some of the fields building steely house on the sacred ground of his ancestors, all in the name of horticultural excellence. The removal of so many hedges so their oversized mechanical machines could take out the trees and clear the ground. The land now infertile, dead, blackened, the wildlife challenged and dismissed. Every crop planted wilted and died, the days of rain in the winter flooded the plains and further degraded the ground. They never understood the need for hedgerows, trees and irrigation, their mind only full of greed and profit.

Larette would never go to the northern quarter, she hated what the humans had done, she prefered the fertile grounds of the Longshoot, Brindley copse and sharply Hollow. These were the places where the trees were strong, lush green pastures clear running streams and rivers, all full of life. The area around the Longshoot was rugged, difficult to negotiate, the terrain was hard but the reason for the unspoilt beauty of the area.

A noise from the forest unnerved her, it was normally quiet and peaceful,

"Hello, who's there? I can handle myself you know." Larette blurted out.

"Handle yourself, I have to agree, what are you doing here so early?" Audrey said, coming out of the undergrowth.

"Oh, it's you."

"Well who did you think it was? I am surprised you couldn't smell me." Giggling out loud.

"Nobody, it is just normally it is quiet here, especially this early."

"Not for much longer."

"What do you mean, much longer, the humans are not coming are they?"

"No, not humans, but some new tenants for Ben Dellies cave, have you not heard, a group of animals crossed the swamp some days ago, it is rumoured they are settling up at the cave."

"But that is grandad's cave!"

"Not anymore, the Wolf of Liberty has given the cave to them, and!"

"And what? don't keep me in suspense."

"Well it is a young bear, about your age, they were forced to move following the red mist."
"I heard about that, nasty, and he lost his mum."

"That be it, his dad listen."

"Well come on, I am dying to know."

"His dad is Scar, you know, the bear that humans hunt, he hates the humans, not unlike you."

"Oh, I wonder what he is like, could do with a bear my age, to be friendly with."

"Only friendly, oh."

"Don't be silly, I don't even know him yet."

"We will see."
With that Audrey slipped in to the undergrowth and was gone.

Larette was excited, she had not seen another bear, for, well ever. But she was determined to assist them when they get there. She went to the spring in the middle of the copse, her thirst needed to be quenched, and this spring offered the most coolest most tasty water ever. It was said that the water from this spring at this time of the day had healing properties like no other. It was just a tale but it was the most tasty water ever. She located the spring which lay aside the tallest tree in the copes, she was just about to take a sip when, Belfor, a wise badger sat watching her.

"Hello Belfor, what brings you here?"

"Same as you, thirst."

"Oh, well it is scrummy."

"Have you heard?"

"Heard what, why is everyone so cryptic."

"Your grandad's place, it is soon to be occupied."

"Oh yes, Audrey mentioned that."

"Well this young bear, has a dipsy friend called Limpy, I have heard of him, Heronetty popped over some time ago, they like to discover places, but they don't like humans, not unlike you."

"That's the second time I have heard that, what am I flavour of the month."

"Flavour of the month, who would eat you?"

Belfor laughed out loud.

"Look, I have to go, but if you see the bear, be nice, you never know."

"Never know what?"

A wink from his eye brought a grin upon her face, but she was worried that there may be some matchmaking going on, even before she had met the bear.

Meanwhile over where Jobe and his friends were, the realisation that soon they would be at their new home, began to flourish. Jobe once again was the last to cross the remaining open space, as he arrived at Brindley Copse, the remaining obstacle was a small river, that needed to be crossed, luckily the storm of a few days ago had brought down a tree that now spanned the river. They all crossed safely, nobody wanted an early morning swim, well except Bonso who dived in to cross to the other side. They all sat down for a well earned rest, it had been a long trek and at last the end of the line was close. There was a strange eeriness that filled the copse, the mist curled round the trunks of trees and silenced any noise from within, but they were almost at their new home.

"Right we can rest a while, at the other end of this river is the Longshoot, our new home. Now we have to be open to what may lie ahead, we can scout the area to find the best place for everyone in the next few days, Bonso no doubt will be somewhere by the river, we will pass Pondlea, and follow the stream to the Longshoot, it will be steep I guess but we need to settle in well before the winter sets in, it is a few months so we should be ok." Jobe said as the other listened but also looked round, getting a bearing to where they were.

Larette sauntered back to Sharply Hollow, unaware that Jobe and his friends had already arrived at Brindley Copse. The sun had begun to burn off the early morning mist as she strolled back.

"Mum, what's for breakfast?"

"Fish, why!"

"Oh, because I am hungry."

"You went out early, was it a nice stroll to the copse?"

"Audrey and Belfor were both about."

"At least you had friends with you!"

"Yes, just the fact they were annoying."

"Annoying, why would they annoy you?"

"No reason, guess it was early in the morning. It was strange though, the mist hugged the trees and it was quite cool."

"Well Autumn is here, and soon Winter."

"I know, Winter."

Larette eat her breakfast, still wondering about the dreams she had been having, and the things she had been told about. Maybe soon she will meet the new bear and his friends but it could take time as winter will soon be upon them.

Jobe and Bonso lead the way, as they reached Pondlea, Bonso just had to dive in for another swim, it had been a long exhaustive trip, but all the rest of the colony freshened up at the side of the Pond. They all had a nice wash and there was a rejuvenated sense of achievement for all of them. The mist had all but gone, in front lay the face of the Longshoot. A tree lined arbour from Pondlea to the Longshoot gave ample cover for all of them, once they got to the Longshoot a brief climb saw them arrive at their new home. The whole group huddled together, they all surveyed the surrounding area from the height of the Longshoot. It had been a long journey, but at least now they could realise their new home and make a wonderful life. Jobe Looked around for the cave that the Wolf of Liberty had mentioned, but it was not at present visible from where they stood. Jobe needed to find the cave before nightfall so they could all rest safely.

Back at Sharply Hollow, Ben Delly asked Larette to fetch him something from his cave, he had forgotten it and wanted to retrieve it before the new tenant arrived. She set out unaware that Jobe and his friends were already there. She took a brisk walk to the Longshoot, the mist had lifted and the smell of the Autumn filled the air, the sun shone through broken cloud as she travelled to the Longshoot. She neared the Cave from the steep side of the hill, then she became aware of some chatter that echoed cross the forest. She was well able to defend herself as her father had made sure she could look after herself, but she stayed low just in case. Seeing the cave was clear she popped in to retrieve Ben Delly's sentimental keepsake. The Chatter intrigued her, she slowly walked round the hillside, quietly she wanted to see what all the chatter was. It was Limpy who saw her first, which startled him,

"A bear, a bear, quick run and hide, it's a bear." Limpy ran behind Jobe.

Jobe spun round to where larette now stood in the shadows,

"Hello Jobe, I heard you were coming, and Limpy, they said you were funny."

"Who said I was funny, I don't know you."

"I'm Larette, I live a few miles that way, Ben Delly is my grandfather, who gave up his cave for you Jobe."

"I hope he is not put out, it wasn't my idea."

"No, he is fine, you are fine, sorry will be fine, just don't be a stranger, oh, and the cave, it's round there."

"But you are a stranger, I haven't seen you before." Jobe answered.

"How adorable, look I have to get back, Ben Delly wants this."

With that she turned and was gone into the forest.

"Jobe, Jobe, what do you think?"

"Think, think about what?"

"Larette, obviously."

"Don't know what you mean."

"Jobe's in love, Jobe's in love." sang Limpy.

"Don't be silly Limpy, I don't know her, yet."

"Are yet, mmm."

Jobe shrugged his shoulders and went to find the cave.

"We can all stop in here tonight, we can have a good look round tomorrow, we need to get settled in, starting tomorrow."

Jobe cast a glance over towards where Larette had gone, unaware she was closer than he thought, then she went home.

They all went to find food and water together as a group, but Jobe was intrigued about Larette, he had not seen any other bears as such.

They all enjoyed their food and set up for the night, now the journey, a very long journey had concluded, it was time to settle in. Their tired hearts and bodies huddled in the cave as night fell, it had been a long arduous journey and now they had the task to set up a new home for all concerned.

Chapter 9

Getting Settled

The sun filtered through the cave entrance, Jobe and the colony had enjoyed their first night in their new home. Jobe, pleased with the fact they could all now rest, after such a long journey, the real task now was to make sure they settle in before the Winter. He Stood at the entrance and looked across the outstretched landscape, the tops of the trees very visible, being so high up, it afforded him a view for many miles. In the distance the outline of Sharply Hollow glimmered in the early morning sunshine. To the left was the steep side of the Longshoot, the undergrowth thick the ground rugged, the forest lined up to offer cover should the need arise, an escape route into the unknown.

"Come on then, let's go and survey our new home, we have a purpose now to build a community, that will thrive and we are safe. Today is the start of our new life, the old one unfortunately has to now remain in the past. It was a traumatic evacuation and the red mist took friends and relatives but we are safe, it is up to us to build our new life, our new community and thrive." Jobe said.

"I have decided that my new home will be at pondlea, it is tranquil and quiet, but not far from you all." Bonso announced "I need to build a home and a dam build build build, summer is nearly over and winter will soon be here."

With that Bonso set off to Pondlea, the rest followed Bonso, it was all new to them and in order to be safe sticking together was paramount. They all assisted Bonso to collect small branches and sticks so he had the material to build his dam and home. After a while Bonso had enough to keep him busy for days, with that they rested then they followed Jude. She was looking for her new home, it needed to be soft top soil and sturdy undersoil in order to build her tunnels, there needed to be few rocks as there was a need to build an extensive tunnel system.

Jobe and Jude looked for a suitable area for the home, well the burrows, they followed the stream to where it erupted from the ground, there was a need to ensure she was not too close to the spring. As they passed the spring the undergrowth thickened a little and only a few trees were in the area, it was away from the spring, there were some small mounds which gave ample cover.

"Jobe, I think this will be ideal, look it is soft the undersoil is compact and the mounds will give added cover if needed."

"As long as you are happy Jude, but can I help you in any way?"

"Not really, it is something I need to do alone, get my planning done and start to burrow." Jude began almost immediately and Deacon and Limpy were the next to look for a suitable place, jobe walked through the bushes and small trees to look for a place for both Deacon and Limpy, possible they would be close together as they could assist each other, though Deacon may need some time away from Limpy, but he had got better.

They found some disused burrows, and together they investigated them, the entrances were a bit shabby but once some of the rubble was cleared away it was evident these would be fine, with a little work on them.

It was the first full day at their new home, everyone seemed so very busy, Jobe felt a bit deflated as they all wanted to be alone to construct their own homes. As they were all so busy Jobe decided he needed to have a general clean up in the cave. He used to help his mother, and the thought of her passing made him a little sad. He remembered the brief speech earlier, life did carry on, no matter what happened in the past, but it had to remain in the past, for everyone's sake.

Jobe found a straight piece of branch and some smaller trigs, binding them together with ivy from the forest. He constructed a brush and swept out the cave, the bedding was removed and then swept away. He collected some new bedding and changed the cave to ensure he felt this was his new home. Once his clean up had concluded he decided to check up on the rest of them, see how they were getting on.

Jude was well advanced with her entrance and he called out, there was no reply, she was obviously busy and Jobe didn't want to disturb her. Limpy and Deacon were almost neighbours and had cleared the burrows out and were adding their own stamp on each home.

Jobe wandered through the arbour of trees on his way to see Bonso. He had made a start on the dam, but he had a lot of work still to do, Jobe didn't want to delay him, after all he needed a house.

Jobe took a drink from the pond, all the sweeping had given him a thirst, and one that needed quenching.

A rustle from the undergrowth startled him,

"Hello, who's there?" Called Jobe,

"Hello Jobe," Larette emerged from the undergrowth.

"Hello, fancy seeing you here."

"Oh Joy, a chat up line."

"A chat up line, what's one of those?" Jobe replied.

"Don't worry, I know a better drinking place than this dirty pond."

"It's not that dirty." Jobe said.

"It is when you see where I drink from!" Larette replied.

"Well, I am unfamiliar with this place, why don't you show me.?"

"With pleasure, just follow me!"

Jobe followed Larette through the forest, they didn't speak a lot, Jobe was unsure what to talk about, after all they had only just met. It was a pleasant walk , Jobe took notice of where they were going , just so he could get back.

"How far is this drinking place, seems a long way just for a drink." Jobe asked.

"Well nice to hear you speak, it is not far now, you are inpatient!" Larette replied.

"Inpatient, what does that even mean?" He said.

"It is when you expect something without waiting! Look we are here." Larette pointed to a small pool, then went over and took a sip.

"Go on then, try the water."

Jobe came over to the pool and sipped the water. It was clear and cool, not much taste but nice.

"What do you think? Jobe, nice or what."

"Hmm, nice cool and clear." he replied.

A rustle in the undergrowth, startled them both.

"Quick hide behind me," Jobe said.

"Why would I hide?"

"It may be humans."

Just then Audrey came out from the undergrowth.

"Oh it's you, should have smelt a rat." Larette said.

"She's not a rat! Is she?" jobe replied

"No, actually I am a skunk, but a very nice one. Isn't that right Larette?"

"Yes Audrey, quite right."

"I see you have met Jobe, thought that might interest you."

"How does she know my name?"

"We all knew you were coming, some time ago. That is why Ben Delly came to Larette, he is her granddad."

" I hope he didn't mind?" Jobe said.

"Anyway, what bring you here Audrey?"

"I just wanted a drink that is all."

"Oh, and we just happened to be here."

"Yes of course."

A gruff voice came from behind, and all three were startled.

"Is this a party, or is this a party?" Belfor said.

"Party, there is no party, we all just need a drink." Larette said.

"Belfor, I guess you knew we were coming too."

"Dear boy, everyone knew you were coming, you're a brave bear to negotiate the swamp, wouldn't catch me there."

Belfor answered.

"But we needed to cross it, to save time, as you know the season's getting old." Jobe said.

"That it is, soon the Winter will be upon us, and everyone needs to be ready, besides the Winter starts earlier in these parts." Belfor said.

"Oh Belfor, you are a drama queen!" Audrey said.

"Drama queen, how can he be a queen? You maybe, but not him." Jobe replied.

They all laughed but time was getting on and Larette needed to get back home, as did Belfor and Audrey.

Jobe wandered back to the cave, he took Belfor's words to task, and began to gather food and store it where he could. True they were further up the mountain and they had no idea what the Winter would bring to the Longshoot.

A new morning gave the colony some time to reflect on their journey, it was a worry as the season grew older but Jobe and his friends were ready for the challenge.

"Gather round, right, we need to get ready for the Winter. I spoke to Belfor, a very knowledgeable Badger round these parts. We need to get set for a long hard and cold Winter, so, plenty of bedding and food stores wherever we can find them, that way we should survive. It will be colder than it was last year, due to the height of the mountain and the northerly position. We have new friends which you will all meet soon, concentrate on the main survival things like food and water, ensure that you will all be warm, we have no idea how bad the Winter will be. Keep bedding clean and dry and plenty of it, you need to keep warm."

"Is Larette coming round later?" asked Bonso.

"Larette will be popping round at times but it is a long trip here from Sharply Hollow, not sure when though. Audrey, a skunk will also pop round as will Belfor, he will help us to ensure we are prepared for the cold Winter." Jobe said.

"Skunk's, they smell don't they?" Deacon asked

"Only if you upset them, so Limpy button it when you see her. Remember that the Wolf of Liberty told us to treat new friends with care and kindness, so maybe less of Skunks smell. They have been here many seasons and we must trust their word as this, our new home, is all very new to us." Jobe's words echoed across the forest right to its edge and they all set to work preparing for Winter.

The next few weeks were to be busy, Jobe wasn't used to preparing for the Winter, his mother did this as he was too young. Larette came visiting on a few occasions some unscheduled, but due to the onset of night, the time was limited, the days were short. Belfor visited all the colony to give some advice on how to survive the Winter. On the day he came to visit Limpy and Deacon, he told them a tale of an old rabbit called Fluff. Now Fluff was a shy fellow and didn't have many friends. He would fill his day with drawing, this was in a cave some way in the distance, he would draw till late in the evening, once he started he couldn't stop, till it was completed.

"Belfor, where was this cave?" Limpy asked "I would one day love to visit it."

"Now that lies in the north, about a mornings walk, but don't go alone, and make sure you know the way back. There is another tale, one I will tell you, soon, of the plight of one such hare. One of your type, who didn't heed the warning, and well, that is for another day."

As they bid goodnight to Belfor the evening was chilly, the heat of the summer had almost passed, a cool and refreshing breeze indicated the onset of Autumn, some of the trees had already started to lose their leaves. The days were full of cloud, the sun on the very occasional visit was a welcome sight, but the days were short and the nights were cold.

Jobe and Larette met in the forest, the drinking spring was cold and the weather was getting the same.

"Larette, are Winter's here cold and unforgiving?" Jobe asked.

"Last year was ok, Ben Delly said that every few years the Winter's were so so cold. I have heard him tell of snow higher than the houses in the village, well not in the village but in this area, the villages are warmer than the mountains, so you will need to keep warm. Me, I like the cold days, I love to walk in the snow and see the pretty patterns left following a hoar frost."

"What is a hoar frost?"

"That is when the windows are coated with frost and just to see the intricate patterns is great, then there is the waterfalls, they have been known to freeze and that is a sight to see."

"Wow, I have never seen the snow that high but we normally sleep through the winter. I was young and mum kept things warm for me and wouldn't let me out in the snow. I think back at Columbus Ridge all the animals played in the snow, the fir trees were decorated but I never saw them. It will be a hard Winter, you know, without mum, and Dad is too far away to come visit now, he used to come on certain days but now we are miles away and I am unsure when I will see him next."

"You will be fine, I will try come and see you, but in the Winter mum don't like me to venture too far in the snow. 'No place for a young cub', she'd say, but I love the snow it is so pure, I sneak out on occasion to play, but if she was to find out, I would be in trouble."

"She is only looking out for you, that what mums do, you need to be looked after."

"Oh, are you offering?" Larette laughed.

"I would look after you, yes."

"How sweet." Larette ruffled his hair."

"Mum used to do that, sometimes I miss her, but we have to carry on, the colony depends on me now."

"Yes I know, just be careful, if you do need help, ask. It will be challenging, the onset of Winter in a new home."

"I will, ask that is."

With that Larette set off back home, as the day grew old, it had been a good day. Jobe had enjoyed the chat with Larette, and the memories shared of his mother.

Jobe sat at the entrance to the cave and looked out across the forest, he remembered when he comforted his mother after the annual hunting day, kept close. Jobe rubbed his head, his heart was aching, the memories bounced across the forest, he watched the shooting stars through the broken clouds of a Autumn's night, each star followed by a wish. The moon through the broken clouds of Autumn lit the forest up. Soon Winter would be here and the snow and cold will engulf the mountains, the night owls echoed, it was surreal, but the calming sounds bounced across the forest.

—— **Chapter 10** ——

The Snows of Winter

The next few weeks passed quickly, Jobe and his friends all now felt this was their home, The Longshoot. New friends Larette, Belfor and Audrey all popped in for a chat, they also joined in the fun at times, but the days were short and cold.

Jobe took a stroll through the forest, initially on his own, but as he progressed through the forest other joined him, it seemed that everyone had the same idea. The trees that had leaves left on them were like a multi coloured ocean in the cool northerly breeze.

"Jobe." Arco said, "What will the Winter bring us, will we still be able to play?"

"Arco, I can't really answer that question, truth is, I don't know. We managed back at Columbus ridge. Though it was lower than where we now reside, the altitude will make it colder no doubt. Belfor did say that every couple of years much snow falls on the mountains in these parts which could make it tricky."

"What do you think the difference in altitude is, compared to the ridge?"

"Well, not quite sure, but we didn't see so many tree tops at the ridge, we can see for miles on a clear day, so that means we are higher."

"Deacon and I seem to be very warm in our burrows, maybe it won't be as cold as we think." Limpy said.

"That's as may be, but wait till you get snowed in!"

"Snowed in, what does that mean? Snowed in."

"It means that your entrance is blocked and covered in deep snow. Freezing outside and not that warm inside either."

"I don't like snow that much." Limpy said.

"Let's just wait and see what happens, shall we!"

A rustle from the undergrowth signalled others were joining the group.

"Larette, how are things with you?"

"Ok, I think, what's this little pow wow?" She asked.

"Well I came out for a stroll, and it seems that everyone had the same idea."

"Well it is a nice day, the trees are so beautiful, full of colour, pastel shades, can you smell the Autumn?"

They all sniffed the air.

"I think that is the normal forest smell, pine nuts and rotting foliage." Limpy said.

"Well I can smell the Autumn, and soon the Winter."

"What does the Winter smell like then?"

"You will know when it is here, the cold freezing air takes your breath away." Larette commented.

"Takes your breath away, won't we die then? I don't want to die yet."

"No Limpy, it's a figure of speech, like a shock or startling feeling." Larette seemed confident in her answer.

"Well I have to go, things to do people to see." with that Larette walked away.

"Who are you seeing?" Limpy asked.

The whole group sniggered, although he had calmed down his silly singing, he was still a scatter brain.

As Larette turned away, Jobe decided to tag along for a while, it had been some time since last they spoke, although time was against them, a companion to walk for a while was a comfort.

"Jobe's in love, Jobe's in love." Limpy Sang.

An awkward backwards glance signalled a disapproving Jobe. Larette giggled but didn't say anything.

"I spoke to soon, thought your singing days were over?" Bonso said.

"They are."

"What was that then?" Bonso said.

"Don't worry, Jobe knows me, he will be fine."

Bonso lead the group back to the Longshoot whilst Jobe and Larette took a quiet stroll through the forest, homeward bound.

"It will be a difficult time for you, Winter, and I doubt we will be able to see each other as much or at all, depending on the snow." Larette said.

"I know, but you never know it may be a mild Winter, you get them every now and then."

"That would be a bonus, for you, as you are just settling in."

"Yes it would be a bonus."

"So you could then see me more!" Larette winked.

"Well yes of course, it's nice to have another bear, to do things with, it can be lonely and now mum's gone, dad's far away, I like spending time with you."

"Is that a fact!"

"Yes it is actually." Jobe answered.

"Look, I have to get back, it will soon be dark and I don't want to worry mum."

"Yes I know that feeling, I used to worry my mum, not on purpose, time just passed by so quickly, and we were having fun. Take care Larette, I need to get back too!"

Jobe said farewell, a backward glance together seemed apt, then it was homeward bound.

The following day, Jobe decided to have a little game with Limpy, following his awkward singing outburst.

"Limpy, can I have a word?"

"Yes Jobe, what can I do for you?"

"Well following your outburst yesterday, Larette is so very upset, she will be informing her dad, of what you did, wouldn't want to be in your shoes?"

"Shoes, I don't wear shoes besides they would not fit you. It was only a bit of fun, you know that."

"I do but Larette didn't did she? Larette is very upset, so what are you going to do to put this right?"

"Put it right, I didn't think it was wrong."

"She is a friend, well was, I am hurt Limpy very hurt. What did I say when we first got here?"

"I can't remember what you said, how can I put it right?"

"Deacon, what do you think? A fitting punishment for Limpy." Jobe winked at Deacon.

"Well Jobe, that is a difficult one, a fitting punishment for what Limpy has done, mmm. I know, he can go and apologize to the Wolf of Liberty, and if he is hungry, the wolf, that is, well I don't fancy his chances, do you!"

"Exactly what I thought, so there you have it, your punishment Limpy. The wolf lives in the barn near the village back a few days trek, and if he accepts your apology, then you will return, if not, well, you know the answer to that one." Jobe said.

"I don't want to go to the barn or see the Wolf, he'll eat me, that is what they do, eat hare."

"Well that is what has been decided." Jobe said.

"But, but," Limpy began.

"Not singing then! What a shame, it's a long walk."

Limpy's head bowed, he turned to commence the journey, then Jobe and Deacon both burst out laughing. Limpy turned before realising what they were up to, and breathed a sigh of relief, he really didn't want to go and see the Wolf.

"Jobe, I am sorry, I will be more careful next time." Limpy said.

"There better not be a next time."

"OK Jobe, sorry."

With that the friends enjoyed the day as the Winter drew ever closer.

The clouds gathered nightly as the winter drew ever closer, each morning the frost painted strange patterns on the puddles left by early evening showers. The rain slowly turned to sleat, and that was significant, as it was the onset of Winter. On the peaks of the Longshoot significant snow showers painted the views of the peak in a white clarity, this was exciting but also worrying. The lower areas had begun to get a coating of snow, which was usual at this time of the year. Larette popped over as the snow showers became more frequent, but she had to be careful, one significant snowfall could impact her return home towards Sharply Hollow.

"Larette." Her mother said, " Maybe you stay close for now, the frequency of the snow showers is becoming more apparent, stay close please."

"Yes mum, I will, but I am just going for a short walk, I won't be long."

"Make sure you are not caught out."

"Mum, I am fine, besides it's not the middle of Winter is it."

"No, but as you well know the weather can change in minutes."

"I can look after myself you know, so don't worry."

Larette was intent on one last visit to see Jobe, after all it could be a long winter.

"Jobe, are you in?" Larette called out.

"Larette, what are you doing here, your mother will be worried, and the weather is unpredictable to say the least."

"Don't fuss, I know what the weather can be like, it's fine."

"Ok, come in, it is not warm outside." Jobe said.

"I like what you have done with the place, all cosy and warm, plenty of food , I think you will be fine over Winter."

"I hope so, I have checked all the homes, it is quite new to most of them, maybe they are not used to the snow, but we will see."

"Neither are you, apparently it wasn't as cold over at the ridge, and your mother, well she looked after you."

"I know but all we can do, is see what happens over the Winter, anyway, it's been a while, as the weather is, maybe you think about getting back. Wouldn't want your mother to worry or be mad at me."

"I know, so maybe yes, time to get back."

Jobe walked Larette to the cave entrance, they were both surprised, the snow had been falling for a while and a vicious wind had whipped up the snow,

"Oh, maybe I shouldn't have come, I don't want to get lost, and mother will be so mad with me."

"It is an issue, I wouldn't want you to get lost, and if both of us go, we could both be lost."

"But mum will be worried, and dad."

"Look best stay here, I will send word to your mother via the forest, explain the reasons why and where you are."

"Send word, but how?"

"Leave it with me, go and sit by the fire and keep warm."

Jobe Ventured out into the snow, it was quite deep, and difficult to walk against the wind. Luckily in the trees by the side of the cave there was a snowy owl's nest, one he knew was occupied, Jobe threw small stones at the nest.

"Whitely, Whitely, I need your help." Jobe shouted.

"Jobe, what on earth are you doing, what is all the noise about?"

"I need you to help me, Larette is stranded here till the snow subsides, can you let her mother and father know that she is fine till the snow subsides and that I will walk her back myself when I can."

"Seriously, it is freezing cold!"

"I know but her family will be worried, I don't want them to be."

"Ok, seeing as it is you."

With that Whitely set off across the forest to inform Larette's family.

Jobe got word back that the message had been delivered and that they were fine with it.

Jobe and Larette settled down to ride out the storm, Jobe knew that once the snow had subsided he would need to explain to Larette's parents the reason for her remaining at the cave. But that was for another day, one that may be a while coming. They settled down together to ride out the first snow of Winter.

The End

Now Winter's Over
Emerging Together

The storm had raged for nearly two weeks and the snow had built up significantly. Following a few days of warmer weather and the lack of that vicious wind the snow had melted enough to venture out.

Larette and Jobe emerged from the cave together, and Bonso and Deacon just happened to be walking by at that exact moment, this gave the colony plenty to talk about.

The first in this series of books 'Columbus Park' is now available at Amazon with the choice of E-book and Audio book for those with limited sight.

A new and exciting book from the Chronicles of Nutwood Grove series will be available shortly. 'A Perilous Summer' follows the first two books 'Fun in The Snow ' and 'Floods of Thaw' all available from Amazon. Valeant is vicious battle for the meadows is also available.

For those who like poetry, 'Timeless Euphoria' a beautiful book of photographic excelence and warming words of comfort is also available. Check out Brandnewwriters.com a site developed for new writer and their work giving them the chance to display their work in a high street store.

www.ingramcontent.com/pod-product-compliance
Lightning Source LLC
Chambersburg PA
CBHW081358090726